A NOTE FOR PARENTS AND EDUCATORS

Terri Bull's Daily Affirmation and Problem Solving Guide was ⟨⟩ between parents/teachers/counselors and their children/students/patients *(little moos)* regarding the best way to resolve conflicts and overcome challenges in a healthy and positive, *"Terri Bull"* way by asking the question, *"What Would Moo Do?"*

Affirmations play a crucial role in helping children develop a strong sense of self-confidence, resilience, and optimism. By incorporating affirmations into their daily routines, parents, educators and counselors can help children build a solid foundation for future success. These concepts are communicated by **Terri Bull**, a lovable character who defies all odds with his unwavering optimism, ingenuity and integrity.

"What Would Moo Do?" goes beyond mere words by presenting over 70 engaging challenges to stimulate critical thinking and problem-solving abilities in children aged 5-11. Each challenge is accompanied by a simple solution of Terri's, prompting children to explore different perspectives and develop their own innovative solutions. Terri's guide provides journaling space for children to put into words their own unique solutions or thoughts on each affirmation or challenge presented to them.

Teaching independent and positive-based problem-solving skills to 5-11 year olds is essential for their personal growth, academic success, and overall well-being. By instilling these skills early on, we empower our children to become confident, resilient, and capable individuals who are prepared to tackle whatever challenges life may bring in a positive and loving way.

Upcoming Terri Bull Adventures you may be interested in!

Be Proud Not Cowed
The Terri Bull School Day
The Terri Bull Sick Day
The Terri Bull Tooth Ache
The Terri Bull Vacation
The Terri Bull Circus Clown

Available in the future on Amazon

*To Kim & Pat ~
For their lifetime of loving,
educating children
and tolerating those of us
who just act like little kids.*

Andrew

No part of this publication may be reproduced in whole or in part, or stored in a retrieval system, or transmitted in any form or by any means, electronic, mechanical, photocopying, recording, or otherwise, without written permission of the publisher. For information regarding permission, visit terribulladventures.com.

ISBN: 979-8-89372-743-2

Copyright 2024 - by J. Andrew deLeon. All rights reserved. This edition is published by Terri Bull Adventures and Jade Marketing & Technology Corporation.

Printed in the U.S.A.

HELP TERRI'S MOM,
MOOCHELLE, RESCUE TERRI.
FILL IN ONE STAR FOR EVERY
COMPLETED JOURNAL PAGE!

Then celebrate with some cookies and MILK!

MY NAME IS

MY PARENT/TEACHER/COUNSELOR IS

What Would Moo Do?

In the pages of
"What Would Moo Do?"
you will find,
A book for young Moos
and each growing young mind.

With Terri Bull leading
through thick and through thin,
The affirmations abound
from the start to the fin.

Oh, what a joy!
In this book, you will see,
A chorus of "I can!"
and a dance of "I'll be!"

The children, they read
and then they all chant,
"I am strong, I am brave!"
with no hint of "I can't."

In this rhythm of words
where their confidence grows,
You'll find little Moos
where the Can-Do River flows.

And in this vibrant land
where self-belief is the key,
Echoes Terri Bull's cheer,
"Be the best you can be!"

With journal in hoof,
and a brisk, hopeful stare,
Terri shows children everywhere
they too can all dare.

And so in each heart,
and in each tiny young hand,
Lies the power to shape,
both to mold, and expand.

Their world of dreams,
under skies vast and true,
Where each one will whisper,
"Oh, What Would Moo Do?"

They face all their fears
with a mighty Moo "Boo!"
And learn that they're more
than they ever once knew.

With Terri Bull's guidance
through each affirmation,
The kids jot and journal
their self-celebration.

"I am kind," "I am smart,"
and "I'm one of a kind!"
Are the powerful words
that will stick in their mind.

"What Would Moo Do?"
asks Terri with glee,
And the answer comes back –
"Be the best Me I can be!"

With pages that turn
and affirmations to say,
This isn't just reading,
it's brightening the day!

For every wee child
who's been feeling quite small,
Comes the words of Terri Bull
to uplift one and all.

Yes, "What Would Moo Do?"
is more than just fun,
It's a boost to the spirit,
a warm, cheerful sun.

It nurtures, it blossoms,
it opens a door,
To a world where a child
can and will be much more.

Written by
Andrew de Leon

Copyright 2024 by J. Andrew deLeon. All rights reserved.
This edition is published by Terri Bull Adventures.

☆ **I AM LOVED BY MY FAMILY!**

WHAT WOULD MOO DO?

CHALLENGE

Feeling left out at home.

SOLUTION

Suggest doing something everyone can enjoy.

AND SO, LITTLE MOOS,
OUR TALE TAKES ITS FLIGHT,
TO CHERISH THE FEELING,
SO SWEET AND SO RIGHT.
UNITE WITH YOUR FAMILY,
SEEK LOVE IN ALL THINGS,
A TREASURE SO PRICELESS,
YOUR HEART TRULY SINGS.

I AM LOVED BY MY FRIENDS!

☆

CHALLENGE

Had an argument with
a friend.

SOLUTION

Apologize and speak calmly
to resolve the issue.

THE MORAL OF THIS STORY
SO GRAND AND SO TRUE,
IS THAT FRIENDS ARE LIKE TREASURES
FOR ME AND FOR YOU!

☆ I AM LOVED BY MY GRANDPARENTS!

_____

_____

_____

_____

_____

_____

_____

_____

WHAT WOULD MOO DO?

CHALLENGE

Feeling sad that your grandparents live far away.

SOLUTION

Call or video chat with them as much as you can.

WITH CREEPING OF TWILIGHT,
WHEN STARS DO APPEAR,
T BULL LISTENS CLOSE,
SO HIS GRANDFOLKS SEEM NEAR.
THROUGH TERRI BULL'S EYES,
WE LEARN WITH EACH FLUTTER,
THAT GRANDPARENTS WHISPERS
MELT HEARTS LIKE WARM BUTTER.

I AM LOVED BY MY TEACHERS!

WHAT WOULD MOO DO?

CHALLENGE

I forgot to do my homework.

SOLUTION

Be honest and ask your teacher for an extension.

THE RHYTHM OF LEARNING,
THE PULSE OF EACH DAY,
IS LOVE AND FORGIVENESS,
IN EVERY WAY.

☆ I AM LOVED BY MY PETS!

_____

_____

_____

_____

_____

_____

_____

_____

_____

WHAT WOULD MOO DO?

CHALLENGE

Feeling scared of a dog.

SOLUTION

Have his owner introduce you.
Be slow, gentle and calm.

HELLO, MR. DOG,
WITH YOUR TEETH SO WHITE,
YOUR BARK SO BIG,
YOUR EYES SO BRIGHT!
I COME IN PEACE,
NO FUSS OR FIGHT!

I AM LOVED BY MYSELF!

WHAT WOULD MOO DO?

CHALLENGE

My friends pressure me into things.

SOLUTION

Trust your instincts. Stand up for what's right.

WHEN CHALLENGES LOOM,
AND THE WORLD SEEMS UNKIND,
REMEMBER, SWEET MOOS,
WHAT'S WITHIN, YOU WILL FIND.
YOUR POWER IS VAST,
YOUR HEART'S FULL OF CHEER,
YOU'RE LOVED BY YOURSELF,
SO NEVER YOU FEAR!

☆ I AM KIND TO OTHERS!

_____

_____

_____

_____

_____

_____

_____

_____

WHAT WOULD MOO DO?

CHALLENGE

My mom came down
with a cold.

SOLUTION

Help bring her breakfast
in bed.

WITH A FLIP AND A FLOP,
TERRI'S PANCAKES TAKE FLIGHT,
ONE LANDS ON HIS HEAD,
TURNING MORNING TO NIGHT.
BUT TERRI'S NOT FLUSTERED,
HE'S FOCUSED, YOU SEE,
OF THE JOY HE'LL IMPART
WITH EACH FLAPJACK, YUMMY!

I AM BRAVE WHEN FACING CHALLENGES!

WHAT WOULD MOO DO?

CHALLENGE

Scared to learn how to swim.

SOLUTION

Take a deep breath and bring an inflatable.

THE POOL IS A SYMBOL
OF LIFE'S GREAT BIG SEAS,
WHERE FEARS EBB AND FLOW
AND YOUR CONFIDENCE FLEES.
TERRI BULL'S SECRET LESSON,
SO GRAND AND SO TRUE—
IT ISN'T THE FEAR,
BUT WHAT BRAVE HEARTS CAN DO.

☆ **I AM SMART AND CAPABLE OF LEARNING NEW THINGS.**

WHAT WOULD MOO DO?

CHALLENGE
Struggling to learn something new.

SOLUTION
Ask for help then practice, practice, practice.

WITH AN OPEN HEART
AND FRIENDS BY YOUR SIDE,
EVERY CHALLENGE YOU MEET,
MAY JUST TURN THE TIDE!
REMEMBER, MY MOOS,
THE ADVENTURE'S BEGUN,
THE WORLD'S FULL OF TREASURES,
OF LEARNING AND FUN.

I AM UNIQUE AND SPECIAL JUST THE WAY I AM. ☆

CHALLENGE

Feeling left out because of different interests.

SOLUTION

Find common ground.
Find like-minded friends.

AS NEW FRIENDS DISCOVER
THE POWER OF PLAY,
WITH EVERY SHARED CHUCKLE,
THEY BRUSH GRAY AWAY.
IN TERRI'S WARM HEART,
WHERE KINDNESS BURNS BRIGHT,
THE SPELL OF TRUE FRIENDSHIP
THE MOST BRILLIANT LIGHT.

☆ **I AM KIND AND CARING.**

WHAT WOULD MOO DO?

CHALLENGE
Witnessing a classmate being teased.

SOLUTION
Offer kind words, then tell a teacher.
.

WHEN STORMS OF TEASING
GATHER 'ROUND,
REMEMBER WHAT TO DO,
JUST SPEAK KIND WORDS
AND STAND UP TALL,
YOUR HEART WILL SEE YOU THROUGH!

I AM BRAVE AND STRONG.

☆

WHAT WOULD MOO DO?

CHALLENGE

Facing a bully on the playground.

SOLUTION

Stand tall with your friends, then tell a teacher or adult.

SO REMEMBER, LIKE TERRI,
WHEN PROBLEMS ARISE,
STAND UP TO YOUR BULLIES,
AND DON'T COMPROMISE.
WITH FRIENDS BY YOUR SIDE,
YOU HAVE NOTHING TO FEAR.
REMEMBER THAT NEXT TIME
DARK SHADOWS LOOM NEAR.

☆ I AM HELPFUL AND THOUGHTFUL!

_____

_____

_____

_____

_____

_____

_____

_____

_____

WHAT WOULD MOO DO?

CHALLENGE

Seeing a friend struggling to carry their books.

SOLUTION

Offer to help carry a few while walking together.

THAT'S QUITE A LOT OF BOOKS DEAR FRIEND,
AND THAT I DO DECLARE!
BUT YES, I HAVE A NOTION,
A SOLUTION FULL OF CARE.
WHY DON'T I LEND A HELPFUL HOOF,
TO EASE YOUR BIG OLE STRAIN?
WE'LL WALK BACK HOME, JUST TWO OF US,
IN SUN OR SLEET OR RAIN!

I AM CREATIVE AND IMAGINATIVE! ☆

WHAT WOULD MOO DO?

CHALLENGE

Feeling bored indoors on a stormy day.

SOLUTION

Create a fort out of blankets and pillows.

.

UNDERNEATH THE PATTER OF THE RAIN,
AND IN THE FLASHLIGHT'S GLOW,
A REALM OF PILLOWS SOFT AS CLOUDS,
WITH SECRET FORTS BELOW.

☆ I AM RESPONSIBLE AND TRUSTWORTHY!

WHAT WOULD MOO DO?

CHALLENGE

Forgot to feed the family pet.

SOLUTION

Apologize, feed & spend extra time with them.

.

I'M SORRY, FURRED BUDDY,
FOR DINNER'S MISHAP,
I'LL FIX IT. I PROMISE,
I WON'T TAKE A NAP.
MORE SNUGGLES, MORE WALKS,
AND A FEAST FOR YOUR TUMMY,
TODAY, YOU'VE MY WORD,
THAT I'LL MAKE SOMETHING NUMMY!

I AM IMPORTANT AND VALUABLE!

WHAT WOULD MOO DO?

CHALLENGE

Feeling unheard when sharing your ideas.

SOLUTION

Speak confidently when expressing your thoughts.

THE TRUTH TERRI LEARNED,
WITH HIS CONFIDENCE FOUND,
WAS SPEAKING ASSURED
WHILE INCREASING THE SOUND
OF HIS VOICE—THOUGH AT FIRST,
A CRACKED, TIMID SMALL SQUEAK—
GREW STRONGER. NOW EXPERTS,
HIS THOUGHTS THEY ALL SEEK.

☆ I AM PATIENT AND PERSISTENT!

_____

_____

_____

_____

_____

_____

_____

_____

_____

CHALLENGE

Feeling frustrated while
learning a new skill.

SOLUTION

Take breaks. Keep practicing
Celebrate progress.

THE LESSON IS CLEAR,
AND IT BEAMS LIKE THE SUN,
PATIENCE AND PRACTICE,
THEY'RE SECOND TO NONE!

I AM RESPECTFUL AND POLITE. ☆

WHAT WOULD MOO DO?

CHALLENGE

Feeling tempted to interrupt someone.

SOLUTION

Wait patiently, listen attentively, speak respectfully!

A WORLD WITH RESPECT,
WHERE WE LISTEN AND HEAR,
EACH VOICE IS A TREASURE,
AND WHISPERS ARE DEAR.
FOR YOUNGEST OF MOOS,
LIFE LESSONS TAKES FLIGHT,
WORDS DO HOLD GREAT POWER,
WHEN YOU USE THEM RIGHT.

☆ I AM HONEST AND FAIR.

CHALLENGE

Tempted to cheat in a game.

SOLUTION

Play fair. Be Honest. Follow the rules.

TERRI LIFTED HIS HEAD,
HIS SMILE IN FULL BLOOM,
FOR HE'D LEARNED A LESSON
INSIDE THAT PLAYROOM.
LIFE'S GAMES ARE MANY,
AND RULES ARE SO CLEAR,
PLAY ALWAYS WITH FAIRNESS,
AND ALWAYS WITH CHEER.

I AM A GOOD FRIEND TO OTHERS.

☆

WHAT WOULD MOO DO?

CHALLENGE

Seeing a friend sitting alone at lunch.

SOLUTION

Invite the friend to sit with your group.

TO BE A GOOD FRIEND,
IS A DEED THAT'S SO GRAND.
IT STARTS WITH A SMILE,
WITH A BIG HELPING HAND.
BY REACHING THOSE WHO
MAY FEEL ALL ALONE,
THE ROOTS OF A FRIENDSHIP
ARE CAREFULLY GROWN.

☆ I AM A GOOD LISTENER.

_____

_____

_____

_____

_____

_____

_____

_____

_____

CHALLENGE

Feeling distracted
during a conversation.

SOLUTION

Maintain eye contact
and turn off the TV.

WITH A NOD AND A WINK,
HIS MISSION, HE KNEW,
WAS TO MASTER THE ART
OF LISTENING TRUE.
TO QUIET ONE'S MOUTH,
TO THINK AND REFLECT,
IS HOW WE GIVE OTHERS
OUR UTMOST RESPECT.

I AM GOOD AT SOLVING PROBLEMS.

☆

WHAT WOULD MOO DO?

CHALLENGE

Feeling overwhelmed by a messy room.

SOLUTION

Make a fun game or a competition out of picking up.

FOR EACH MESSY ROOM
IS A PUZZLE YOU'LL FIND,
A PROBLEM TO SOLVE
WITH YOUR CAPABLE MIND!
KEEP LAUGHTER REAL CLOSE
POSITIVITY HIGH,
YOUR ROOM IS NOW CLEAN
NOT A SMELLY PIG STY.

☆ I AM GRATEFUL FOR THE GOOD THINGS IN MY LIFE.

WHAT WOULD MOO DO?

CHALLENGE

Feeling sad about not getting a new toy.

SOLUTION

Revisit the toys you have and invent new ways to play.

OUR TOYS, REIMAGINED,
TELL ALL OF THEIR TALES,
OF HUGE MOUNTAINS CLIMBED
AND BLACK PIRATE SAILS.
A CHEER, A JOY,
A GRATEFUL HEART,
TO US, IS WHAT
OUR TOYS IMPART.

I AM CONFIDENT IN MYSELF.

☆

CHALLENGE

Feeling unsure about making new friends.

SOLUTION

Approach others with a smile and be yourself.

REMEMBER, SMALL MOOS,
WHEN THE GOING GETS TOUGH,
YOU'RE SUCH A GOOD PERSON;
YOU'RE MORE THAN ENOUGH.
DON'T NEGLECT TO SAY HI,
OR TRY SOMETHING NEW,
THERE'S SO MUCH TO GAIN,
WITH A FRIENDSHIP OR TWO.

☆ I AM LOVED JUST THE WAY I AM.

WHAT WOULD MOO DO?

CHALLENGE
Feeling unloved after making a mistake.

SOLUTION
Remember, love is unconditional. Mistakes happen.

LIFE, LITTLE MOOS,
HOLDS A LESSON SO GRAND,
THAT LOVE'S NOT DIMINISHED,
NOT EVEN A STRAND,
BY THE STUMBLES, THE FUMBLES,
THE MISTAKES THAT YOU MAKE,
LOVE'S VAST AS AN OCEAN,
AND SWEET AS A CAKE.

I AM TALENTED AND UNIQUE!

☆

WHAT WOULD MOO DO?

CHALLENGE

Feeling unappreciated for my unique talents.

SOLUTION

Share talents with enthusiasm. Embrace your uniqueness.

NO MATTER YOUR GIFT,
NO MATTER HOW MEEK,
EVEN UNAPPRECIATED,
IT MAKES YOU UNIQUE.
BE PROUD OF YOUR TALENT,
BE PROUD OF YOUR FLAIR,
FOR YOU ARE UNIQUE,
AND BEYOND ALL COMPARE.

☆ I AM FULL OF ENERGY AND ENTHUSIASM.

WHAT WOULD MOO DO?

CHALLENGE

Feeling antsy during a long car ride.

SOLUTION

Play interactive games or sing along to music.

WITH BOLTS OF ENERGY
FROM YOU MY YOUNG MOO
THERE'S NEVER A CHALLENGE
THAT'S TOO BIG FOR YOU.
PLAY GAMES AND SING SONGS,
FILL THE AIR WITH YOUR VOICE,
AND CAR RIDES WILL BE
BUT A CAUSE TO REJOICE.

I AM CAPABLE OF ACHIEVING MY GOALS.

CHALLENGE

Frustrated and not able to reach my goal.

SOLUTION

Break down your efforts into smaller tasks.

YOU ARE CAPABLE, DEAR MOOS,
BEYOND MEASURE, YOU SEE,
OF CHASING YOUR DREAMS,
WHATEVER THEY BE!
SMALL GOALS OR BIG GOALS,
LIKE STEALING 3RD BASE,
TAKE TASKS STEP BY STEP,
WITH A SMILE ON YOUR FACE.

☆ **I AM PROUD OF MYSELF AND MY ACCOMPLISHMENTS.**

WHAT WOULD MOO DO?

CHALLENGE

Struggling to learn something new.

SOLUTION

Ask for help and never stop trying.

WHEN YOU LEARN SOMETHING NEW,
YOU STRUGGLE AT FIRST,
REMEMBER ONE THING,
THIS ALWAYS COMES FIRST:
"I AM PROUD OF MYSELF,
AS PROUD AS A KING —
WITH HELP AND HARD WORK
I CAN DO ANYTHING.

I AM IMPORTANT AND MAKE A DIFFERENCE IN THE WORLD. ☆

CHALLENGE

Feeling small in a big world.

SOLUTION

Help others. Smile at someone who looks sad.

REMEMBER, SMALL MOOS,
IN YOUR THOUGHTS AND YOUR DEEDS,
YOU'RE IMPORTANT AND STRONG,
WHAT EVERYONE NEEDS.
NO MATTER HOW SMALL
YOU MAY FEEL ON THIS EARTH.
YOUR SMILE GRANTS A SAD CHILD
AMAZING SELF WORTH.

☆ I AM KIND TO ANIMALS AND NATURE.

WHAT WOULD MOO DO?

CHALLENGE
Seeing trash littering a park.

SOLUTION
Pick up. Keep the park clean. Help keep animals safe!

CHILDREN OF EARTH,
TAKE TERRI'S ADVICE,
BY KEEPING PARKS CLEAN
AND EVERYTHING NICE
WE KINDLE OUR LOVE
FOR ALL THAT WE SHARE,
WE KEEP THE WORLD SAFE
AND HELP FRESHEN AIR.

I AM LOVED AND SUPPORTED BY MY FAMILY. ☆

CHALLENGE

Feeling scared after a bad dream.

SOLUTION

Hugs from parents and stuffies bring comfort.

AT TIMES IN THE LAND
OF MOONSHINE AND DREAMS,
ADVENTURES MAY TEAR YOU
APART AT THE SEAMS.
YOUR FEELINGS, FEARS,
AND EVERY FRIGHT,
NEED STUFFIES AND HUGS
TO PREVENT THEM AT NIGHT.

☆ **I AM A GOOD HELPER AT HOME AND AT SCHOOL.**

WHAT WOULD MOO DO?

CHALLENGE

I accidently Spilled my
juice.

SOLUTION

Clean up your spill. Slow down.
Be more careful.

"YOU'RE A VERY GOOD HELPER,"
TERRI'S PARENTS DECLARED,
"JUST PRACTICE SOME CAUTION,
AND YOU WILL BE SPARED
FROM MISHAPS AND MAYHEM,
FROM SPILLS ON THE GROUND,
BY SLOWING IT DOWN
AND JUST LOOKING AROUND."

I AM RESPONSIBLE FOR MY ACTIONS AND CHOICES. ☆

WHAT WOULD MOO DO?

CHALLENGE

I forgot to do my chores.

SOLUTION

Complete your chores before more play time.

IN LIFE, WE HAVE CHORES,
WE HAVE DUTIES TO DO,
BUT THE WAY THAT WE FACE THEM,
IS QUITE UP TO YOU.
BY FACING YOUR TASKS
WITH SOME JOY, LITTLE MOO,
THEY BECOME LOTS OF FUN...
JUST DON'T STEP IN DOG POO.

☆ I AM BRAVE ENOUGH TO TRY NEW THINGS.

_____

_____

_____

_____

_____

_____

_____

_____

WHAT WOULD MOO DO?

CHALLENGE

Feeling nervous about trying a new food.

SOLUTION

Try a small bite. It may be your new favorite!

THOUGH YOUR TUMMY MIGHT ROLL
AND YOUR HEART GIVE A THUD,
ALTHOUGH YOU MIGHT THINK
THAT, "THIS FOOD TASTES LIKE MUD!"
THE TASTE OF THE NEW,
OH WHAT JOY FOR THE BRAVE,
FOR TRYING, YOUNG MOOS,
WE JUST FOUND OUR NEW FAVE!

I AM A GOOD PROBLEM SOLVER.

WHAT WOULD MOO DO?

CHALLENGE

My toys won't all fit in my toy box.

SOLUTION

Arrange toys differently. Donate old toys to the needy.

I'LL SORT ALL MY TOYS,
GIVE A SHOUT OF HURRAY,
WHEN I FIND NEW SAFE PLACES
FOR MY TOYS TO STAY.
FOR THOSE LITTLE MOOS
WHO DID NOT OWN A ONE,
EXTRA TOYS OF T. BULL
WOULD PROVIDE THEM SOME FUN.

☆ I AM RESPECTFUL TOWARDS OTHERS.

WHAT WOULD MOO DO?

CHALLENGE

Taking a toy without asking.

SOLUTION

Apologize and in the future ask permission first!

NEVER TAKE WHAT YOU WANT
WITHOUT HEARING THIS PLEA.
"IF THIS TOY HAD BEEN MINE,
HOW DEPRESSED WOULD I BE?"
WHEN RESPECTING ANOTHER,
YOU RESPECT YOURSELF TOO,
A LIFE LESSON LEARNED,
FOR EACH SMALL HONEST MOO.

I AM GRATEFUL FOR THE LOVE AND CARE I GET. ☆

CHALLENGE

Fighting with a family member.

SOLUTION

Remember they love you. Apologize and make-up.

LOVE IS THE VICTOR,
AND PEACE IS THE PRIZE,
WHEN HUGGING IT OUT,
HEARTS WILL TRIPLE IN SIZE,
BE GRATEFUL FOR LOVE,
IT'S THE BEST WAY TO BE.
WHEN DEALING WITH MEMBERS
OF YOUR FAMILY.

☆ I AM A GOOD PERSON WHO CARES ABOUT OTHERS.

WHAT WOULD MOO DO?

CHALLENGE

You notice that your dog looks sad.

SOLUTION

Cheer them up with a belly rub and ear scratch..

CHEER UP, MY POOCH,
IT'S NOT SO TOUGH,
A HELPING SCRATCH,
THAT'S JUST THE STUFF!
SO SCOOTER JUST HAD
HIS BELLY RUB DREAMS,
NOW NOTHING, DOGGONE-IT,
IS BAD AS IT SEEMS!

I AM FULL OF POTENTIAL AND POSSIBILITIES. ☆

WHAT WOULD MOO DO?

CHALLENGE

Drawing something and feeling stuck.

SOLUTION

Look at it differently. Try out new ideas!

HAVE YOU EVER DRAWN SOMETHING,
FELT STUCK IN A RUT,
HAVING COLORS TO DRAW
BUT YOUR MIND IS ALL SHUT?
JUST EMBRACE YOUR MISTAKES
AND THE CHANGES THEY BRING,
WHEN YOU TRY NEW IDEAS
YOUR RESULTS WILL JUST RING!

☆ **I AM WORTHY OF LOVE AND FRIENDSHIP.**

WHAT WOULD MOO DO?

CHALLENGE

Having my first best friend.

SOLUTION

Remember you are amazing and worthy of love.

TODAY'S A GRAND DAY,
I'VE FOUND MY BEST FRIEND,
OUR DAYS WILL BE AWESOME,
OUR LAUGHS WILL NOT END!
"WE'RE WORTHY," WE WHISPERED,
TO MOON AND THE SKIES,
"IF FRIENDSHIP'S A TROPHY,
WE'VE WON THE GRAND PRIZE!"

I'M CAPABLE OF MAKING A POSITIVE DIFFERENCE.

CHALLENGE

Seeing a garden with dying flowers.

SOLUTION

Water the garden and watch the plants grow and thrive.

OUR TERRI, PERPLEXED,
SCRATCHED HIS LITTLE BULL-HEAD,
A CHALLENGE SO BIG,
PRETTY FLOWERS NEAR DEAD!
WITH POWERFUL PURPOSE
AND WATER IN TOW,
HE HANDILY SAVED
THE GREEN GARDEN BELOW.

☆ I'M CURIOUS AND LOVE TO EXPLORE THE WORLD AROUND ME.

WHAT WOULD MOO DO?

CHALLENGE

Stuck at home and feeling bored.

SOLUTION

Explore your backyard, discover insects and plants.

WITH EACH CREATURE FOUND,
TERRI BULL BEAMS WITH GLEE,
IN FLORA AND FAUNA,
HE FINDS FAMILY.
ADVENTURES IN BACKYARDS
ARE TREASURES OF FUN,
WHERE EARTH AND ITS CREATURES
SHINE UNDER THE SUN.

I AM STRONG AND RESILIENT. ☆

CHALLENGE

Falling off your bike while learning to ride.

SOLUTION

Brush yourself off. Get back on, and never give up!

HE PEDALED AND WOBBLED,
BUT THIS TIME HE RODE,
AND EVERY NEW SWAY
WAS A SPIN TO BEHOLD.
"YOU DID IT, YOU DID IT!"
THE LITTLE MOOS CRIED,
"IT'S TRYING THAT'S WINNING,"
TERRI BULL JUST REPLIED.

☆ I AM GRATEFUL FOR THE SIMPLE JOYS IN LIFE.

_____

_____

_____

_____

_____

_____

_____

_____

CHALLENGE

Rainy weather cancels your plans.

SOLUTION

Play a favorite board game inside with your family!

YOUR PLANS HAD BEEN SET
BEFORE THIS WEATHER'S TALE,
THE SKIES OPENED UP
AND YOUR PLANS ALL DERAIL.
INSTEAD STAY INSIDE
WHERE THE EMBERS ARE WARM
PLAY GAMES AND MAKE TREATS
AS YOU WAIT OUT THE STORM.

I AM CAPABLE OF ACHIEVING ANYTHING. ☆

WHAT WOULD MOO DO?

CHALLENGE

Struggling to tie your shoelaces.

SOLUTION

Don't give up. Keep practicing, you will get it!

LACES, OH LACES,
THEY WEAVE AND THEY WIND,
AROUND LOOPS AND TWISTS,
A FULL PUZZLE, YOU'LL FIND.
BUT PRACTICE AND PATIENCE
ARE SECRETS YOU'LL LEARN.
FROM WORKING REAL HARD
WHERE BIG KNOTS ARE CONCERNED.

☆ I CARE ABOUT OTHERS' FEELINGS.

WHAT WOULD MOO DO?

CHALLENGE

Seeing a friend alone and crying.

SOLUTION

Comfort them with hugs and kind words.

SO, JUST DOWN THE LANE,
TERRI HEARD A SOFT MOAN.
A FRIEND, WITH HEAD DOWN
IN TEARS ALL ALONE.
WITH A TWIRL AND A WHIRL,
AND A SLIGHT GENTLE SQUEEZE,
KIND WORDS AND WARM HUGS
DID BRING SAD TO ITS KNEES.

I AM CONFIDENT IN EXPRESSING MYSELF. ☆

WHAT WOULD MOO DO?

CHALLENGE

Feeling nervous about sharing an idea in class.

SOLUTION

Take a deep breath and speak confidently.

TEETH CHATTER LIKE MARBLES,
THOUGHTS FLEE YOU LIKE BIRDS,
YOUR CONFIDENCE FALLS
LIKE DISCARDED OLD WORDS.
TAKE A BREATH AND BE STEADY
AND GATHER YOUR NERVE.
ONLY THEN WILL YOU FIND
YOUR HUGE COURAGE RESERVE.

☆ I AM FULL OF CREATIVITY AND ORIGINAL IDEAS.

_____

_____

_____

_____

_____

_____

_____

_____

_____

WHAT WOULD MOO DO?

CHALLENGE
Bored of playing the same old thing.

SOLUTION
Use your imagination to Create your own game with your own rules.

LITTLE MOOS, BE INSPIRED
BY TERRI'S GREAT PLAY,
GO CREATE AND INVENT,
IN YOUR VERY OWN WAY.
FOR IN YOU, DEAR CHILDREN,
MUCH BRILLIANCE JUST DWELLS
TO CREATE A NEW GAME,
WITH NEW RULES AND NEW SPELLS.

I AM BRAVE ENOUGH TO ASK FOR HELP WHEN I NEED IT. ☆

CHALLENGE

Confused about your teacher's lesson.

SOLUTION

Take a deep breath. Raise your hand. Ask for help.

THE ANSWER, PERHAPS,
IS AS PLAIN AS CAN BE,
JUST ASK FOR SOME HELP,
AND SOON YOU WILL SEE.
IN THIS WORLD THAT WE LIVE,
WHERE YOUR FEARS SOMETIMES CREEP,
THERE'S NO MOUNTAIN TOO HIGH
OR NO OCEAN TOO DEEP.

☆ **I AM LOVED FOR WHO I AM, INSIDE AND OUT.**

WHAT WOULD MOO DO?

CHALLENGE

Unsure if others like you for
who you are.

SOLUTION

True friends love you
for your inner you.

BELIEVE IN YOURSELF,
BECAUSE YOU ARE ENOUGH,
WITH COURAGE AND KINDNESS,
YOU'LL CONQUER WHAT'S ROUGH.
YOUR HEART'S FILLED WITH MAGIC,
YOUR SOUL'S BRIGHT AND TRUE,
YOUR BEST FRIENDS WILL LOVE YOU
FOR YOUR INNER MOO.

I AM FULL OF HAPPINESS AND JOY.

☆

WHAT WOULD MOO DO?

CHALLENGE

Feeling stuck inside during a snow storm.

SOLUTION

Bundle up. Go outside. Make snow angels!

IN BOOTS AND MITTENS,
THICK JACKETS, AND ALL,
TERRI WADDLED THROUGH SNOW.
HE WAS HAVING A BALL!
HE FLAPPED HIS LIMBS WIDE,
FLOPPED A DANCE ON THE GROUND,
CREATING SNOW ANGELS,
HIS HAPPINESS FOUND.

☆ **I AM A GOOD SPORT, WIN OR LOSE.**

WHAT WOULD MOO DO?

Being Part of a losing team
or having lost a game.

Congratulate your opponent(s).
Be a good sport.

WHEN THE GAMES THAT YOU PLAY
DON'T QUITE END AS YOU CHOOSE,
THERE'S A WAY TO STILL WIN.
BE A SPORT, AND NOT LOSE.
FOR WINNING'S NOT JUST
WHEN YOU BEAT ALL THE REST.
IT'S ALSO YOUR EFFORT
THAT MAKES YOU THE BEST.

I AM CONFIDENT IN TRYING NEW THINGS. ☆

WHAT WOULD MOO DO?

CHALLENGE

Scared to try out a brand new sport.

SOLUTION

Take a deep breath. Put on your gear. Dive in!

A NEW CHALLENGE BECKONED,
THE SCHOOL'S DIVING TEAM.
A SPORT UP SO HIGH,
IT FELT LIKE A BAD DREAM.
NEW THINGS CAN BE SCARY,
LIKE SHADOWS AT NIGHT.
BUT EACH DARING LEAP,
BRINGS YOU INTO THE LIGHT.

☆ I HAVE A PURPOSE IN LIFE.

_____

_____

_____

_____

_____

_____

_____

_____

WHAT WOULD MOO DO?

CHALLENGE

Feeling unsure about what challenge to take on next?.

SOLUTION

Set a goal and take your first step towards it.

REMEMBER, MY MOO,
HAVE A PURPOSE IN MIND,
WHATEVER YOUR PATH
JUST MAKE SURE YOU STAY KIND.
FOR EVERYONE HERE,
THE TASK SHOULD STAY THE SAME,
SET GOALS, TAKE STEPS,
AND BEGIN A NEW GAME!

I AM FULL OF POTENTIAL AND POSSIBILITIES. ☆

CHALLENGE

Having a friend that speaks a foreign language.

SOLUTION

Teach each other new foreign words and phrases.

IN EVERY HOLA
OR BONJOUR OR CIAO,
LIES WELCOMING HUGS
FOR THIS HAPPY SMALL COW.
WITH NEW FOREIGN PHRASES
UPON BOTH OF OUR LIPS,
WE'RE ALREADY PLANNING
SOME OVERSEAS TRIPS.

☆ **I AM KIND AND GENTLE WITH MYSELF.**

WHAT WOULD MOO DO?

CHALLENGE

Making a mistake on a test at school.

SOLUTION

Mistakes are inevitable and part of the learning process.

MISTAKES ARE JUST LESSONS
IN CLEVER DISGUISE,
SO FORGIVING OURSELVES
IS MOST TRULY QUITE WISE.
BY LEARNING FROM ERRORS
WE MAKE ON A TEST,
WE'VE GAINED IN NEW KNOWLEDGE
THAT MAKES US OUR BEST.

I AM EMPATHETIC AND UNDERSTANDING. ☆

WHAT WOULD MOO DO?

CHALLENGE

See a classmate struggling with schoolwork.

SOLUTION

Be kind and offer to help. Form a study group.

WITH NUMBERS AND FIGURES
SPREAD OUT ON THE GRASS,
THEY TACKLED EACH PROBLEM,
EACH SUM AND EACH MASS.
"FOR EACH TRICKY SUM,
THERE'S AN ANSWER SO SWEET,
A PUZZLE TO SOLVE,
AND A RIDDLE TO GREET."

☆ I AM CONFIDENT IN MY ABILITIES.

WHAT WOULD MOO DO?

CHALLENGE

Feeling anxious about a public performance.

SOLUTION

Believe in yourself, focus on the fun, forget the crowd.

SO TERRI SANG ARIAS,
IN BRIGHT OPERA LIGHT,
A SPECTACULAR VISION,
THIS MAGICAL NIGHT.
THE AUDIENCE FADED,
LIKE SHADOWS AT DAWN.
HIS ANXIOUS MOOO'D MELTED
ONCE CRITICS WERE GONE.

I LOVE UNCONDITIONALLY.

☆

CHALLENGE

Sometimes your family makes you mad.

SOLUTION

Remember to keep loving them no matter what!

WHEN FAMILIES FROWN
AND TEMPERS DO SOAR.
WHEN YOUNG MOOS JUST GRUMBLE
AND SLAM YOUR ROOM DOOR.
REMEMBER LOVE'S BOUNDLESS,
IT SHOULD LEAD THE WAY.
UNCONDITIONAL LOVE,
IS THE LOVE HERE TO STAY.

☆ I SPREAD KINDNESS!

_____

_____

_____

_____

_____

_____

_____

_____

_____

CHALLENGE

A hot and steamy summer
day.

SOLUTION

Invite other kids to play in
your water sprinkler.

OUR HOT STEAMY DAY
BEGINS WITHOUT CHEER.
THE AIR IS SO THICK,
THAT IT'S ALMOST LIKE FEAR.
BUT TERRI IS HERE
TO RESCUE THE DAY,
WITH SPRINKLER FUN
THAT KEEPS HEAT AWAY!

I EMBRACE CHANGE!

CHALLENGE

Moving to a new home or neighborhood.

SOLUTION

Explore, make new friends and join the adventure!

NEW LANDS TO DISCOVER,
NEW JOYS TO UNFOLD,
MORE FRIENDS TO DISCOVER,
MORE STORIES UNTOLD.
THE SECRET TO THRIVING,
WITH LIFE'S REARRANGE,
IS ONE SIMPLE SENTENCE,
"I WILL EMBRACE CHANGE!"

☆ I BOUNCE BACK STRONGER.

_____

_____

_____

_____

_____

_____

_____

_____

_____

CHALLENGE

Feeling sick and missing some school.

SOLUTION

Rest, take your medicine and listen to your doctor.

OUR TALE FINDS OUR HERO,
QUITE UNDER THE WEATHER,
AND SUNNY SCHOOL DAYS?
MISSED THEM ALTOGETHER!
THE BED WHERE HE'S NESTLED,
SOFT PILLOWS AND ALL,
CHICKEN SOUP, YUCKY PILLS
AND HIS DOCTOR ON CALL.

I TRUST MYSELF, AND HANDLE PROBLEMS CALMLY. ☆

WHAT WOULD MOO DO?

CHALLENGE

Getting lost somewhere you've never been.

SOLUTION

Stay calm. Find a safe place. Ask for help.

FOR TERRI BULL
HAD LEARNED THIS DAY,
NO MATTER WHERE
YOU GO ASTRAY.
THE MOO THAT'S CALM
AND TRUSTS HIS WAY,
CAN FIND HIS FOLKS
AND BE OKAY.

☆ I PURSUE MY DREAMS.

_____

_____

_____

_____

_____

_____

_____

_____

_____

CHALLENGE

Failing when trying out something new.

SOLUTION

Keep at it. The only fail is to never try.

WITH EVERY PURSUIT
REMEMBER THIS LINE,
IN CHASING YOUR DREAMS,
YOUR EFFORT MUST SHINE.
PERSISTENCE MUST BE
TURNED UP TO A HIGH
IT'S ONLY A FAIL
IF YOU NEVER TRY.

I LAUGH OFTEN, BRINGING JOY TO OTHERS. ☆

CHALLENGE

Your friends feel sad on a gloomy day.

SOLUTION

Learn some jokes, share a smile and spread some joy.

TERRI HAD TAUGHT THEM
THIS ONE SIMPLE TRUTH,
FOR EVERY DOWN DAY,
THERE'S AN UP DAY, FORSOOTH,
SO EVEN WHEN DAYS
ARE WET, DARK AND GRAY,
A JOKE AND SOME LAUGHTER
MAY JUST SAVE THE DAY.

☆ I INSPIRE OTHERS, WITH MY ACTIONS.

WHAT WOULD MOO DO?

CHALLENGE

Family member are buried with chores.

SOLUTION

Lend a hand. Help without being asked. Lighten their load.

WHEN YOUR FAMILY IS BURIED
IN DISHES AND GRIME,
AND THEIR CHORE LIST IS LONG
AS A TERRI BULL RHYME.
WITH A SMILE AND A SKIP,
YOU CAN LESSEN THEIR TASK,
IF YOU SWOOP IN TO HELP
WITHOUT EVEN AN ASK.

I AM GRATEFUL, FOR ALL MY BLESSINGS.

CHALLENGE

Feeling upset when someone gets a bigger sized gift.

SOLUTION

Sometimes the best gifts come in small packages.

LITTLE MOOS LEARN A LESSON,
YOUR HEART WILL GROW WIDE,
GIFT PRICE DOES NOT MATTER,
BUT LOVE FOUND INSIDE.
WE MUST KEEP THE SPIRIT
OF THANKS IN OUR CORE,
FOR LIFE'S RICHEST GIFTS
ARE NOT FOUND IN A STORE.

☆ I AM A UNIQUE CREATIVE SOUL.

WHAT WOULD MOO DO?

CHALLENGE
Feeling pressured to fit
into a friend group.

SOLUTION
Don't give into peer pressure.
Find friends who think like you.

A GROUP OF OLD FRIENDS PRESSED
T. BULL TO BE RUDE,
WHICH WASN'T A FIT
FOR HIS POSITIVE MOOD.
SINCE ANGER AND MEANNESS
JUST MADE HIM FEEL ILL,
HE WENT OUT, FOUND NEW FRIENDS
MORE KIND AND MORE CHILL.

I LEARN FROM MY MISTAKES.

☆

CHALLENGE

Burning cookies you were baking.

SOLUTION

Make a smaller batch first, then adjust the oven temp.

FROM OUT OF BURNT COOKIES,
A TRIUMPH WE'LL EARN.
WHEN TURNING THE TEMP
OF THE OVEN OFF, "BURN."
NEXT TIME I WILL BAKE
A MUCH LARGER TEST BATCH
AND ENJOY ALL THE COOKIES
MADE BY ME FROM SCRATCH.

☆ **I AM JOYFUL AND FIND HAPPINESS IN LIFE.**

WHAT WOULD MOO DO?

CHALLENGE

Embarrassed after tripping and falling.

SOLUTION

Laugh at yourself, grin and make a joke.

ONE BRIGHT SUNNY DAY,
AS TERRI STROLLED BY,
HE TRIPPED ON A ROOT
FELL INTO A PIE!
INSTEAD OF HIM BLUSHING
AND RUSHING AWAY,
SAID, "FALLING'S JUST DANCING
WITH TWISTS AND A SWAY."

I AM ENOUGH, JUST AS I AM.

☆

CHALLENGE

Insecure feelings of who you are inside.

SOLUTION

Realize what makes you different makes you unique!

"WHAT WOULD MOO DO,"
GAVE YOU AFFIRMATION
TO OPEN YOUR EYES
TO THIS OBSERVATION
OF HOW GREAT YOU ARE
WITHOUT LIMITATION
I HOPE YOU HAVE LOVED
MY PUBLICATION!

JUST SOME

MOOOO-SCELLANEOUS THOUGHTS

Made in the USA
Monee, IL
01 November 2024

69140468R00044